THE LITTLE BOOKS OF BIG BUSINESS

BOOK #1

CAT CASEY
TURNS BROWNIES INTO A BUSINESS

First Edition 2021
Published by Success Street Coaching LLC

Cover Art "Lezhepyoka" @123RF.com
Interior Illustrations by Fiona Reed

CAT CASEY TURNS BROWNIES INTO A BUSINESS

CAT CASEY TURNS BROWNIES INTO A BUSINESS

MARA
WILLIAMS
Illustrations by Fiona Reed

Success Street Coaching LLC

To my parents,
who made reading & learning fun.

First Printing, 2021

My name is Cat Casey and I'm eleven years old. It's fall in my neighborhood and the maple leaves are yellow, green and red. Two days ago I took my biggest order to date; 500 Pumpkin Twinkle Bars for The Blue Moon Cafe on Main Street, for their annual Halloween Spooktacular.

Every year the town businesses on Main Street host a pumpkin carving contest for all ages. Each business along the street sets up a Halloween display in their store window.

The Blue Moon Cafe is the main sponsor. They pay for all the lights inside the display pumpkins. They provide prizes for the best carvings. They also make all the signs and promote the big event.

This year they placed an order for my Pumpkin Twinkle Bars. I have no idea how I am going to deliver their order of five hundred bars on time and by myself.

CHAPTER 1

Selling Pumpkin Twinkle Bars started by accident one month ago. School was back in full swing for the new school year. We were raising money for new costumes for our holiday talent show. Every year people in the town put on a show. It should be on Broadway in New York, or at least off Broadway in a big theater. They always sell-out tickets and end up with standing room only in the back.

My three friends Nick, Emma and Max and I have a talent that started when we were younger. We all lived on the same block. Our families had dinner together every Wednesday night. We called it "Wednesday Winner" for Wednesday Dinner. We thought we were so funny.

Usually we got the job of either setting the table or watching Max and Emma's little brothers to keep them busy while our parents visited and got dinner ready. To entertain the little boys, we made up a routine called The Chin-a-kins. It's called Chin-a-kins because we all lie upside down on a couch to pretend that our chins are the tops of our heads. We tie a scarf or a bandana over our nose and eyes, put little stickers on our chins for eyes and wear little doll hats on our chins. Then we sing songs as the "Four Chin-A-Kins" and make the little boys laugh.

Each week we practiced a new song and even started adding in some jokes from Nick's library joke book. When we were nine, we decided to enter the junior division of the talent show and won "Best New Act". Last year we decided we needed matching scarves for our heads and some props for the routine. We put together a bake sale in our neighborhood and that's where the Pumpkin Twinkle Bar business began.

I was looking for recipes for treats, to make for the bake sale, when I came across an old tin box of recipe cards that was tucked in the very back of our pantry. My mom said they were family recipes and I could look through them. The recipes were for some of our favorites, like the Goofy Cake that my older brother Bobby likes on his birthday. There was the potato salad that my mom makes for 4th of July every year, and there was also one I hadn't heard of before called "Pumpkin Brownie Bars". My grandmother's handwriting was neat and straight and small.

PUMPKIN BROWNIE BARS

6 eggs
1 1/2 cup sugar
1 1/2 tsp vanilla

3 cups flour
3/4 tsp salt
1 1/2 tsp baking powder

Mix all ingredients together with a mixer, starting with the eggs & sugar. When mixed, remove 1 cup of the batter & put it in a separate bowl.

In the separate bowl (with the cup of batter) add:
1 cup (1/2 can) pumpkin puree
1 1/2 tsp cinnamon
1/4 tsp nutmeg

In the original bowl add:
12 TBSP (1 1/2 sticks) softened butter
1 1/2 cup baking cocoa
1/3 cup vegetable oil
1 cup (other 1/2 can) pumpkin puree

- Grease bottom of 9x13 pan with butter
- Spread chocolate mixture in pan
- Spread pumpkin mixture over chocolate
- Sprinkle top with 1/3 bag chocolate chips
- Bake 35-40 minutes at 350 degrees

It is October, so a pumpkin dessert might be a good choice for this time of year. Nick, Emma, Max and I all talked on Wednesday Winner and agreed to each bring one batch of dessert cut into twelve pieces. That way we could sell 48 items for 50 cents each and make $24 during our bake sale. That would give us each $6 to use towards our Chin-a-kins costumes.

I got to work on Saturday making a practice batch of bars. We had everything needed for the recipe except a can of pumpkin, so I added it to my mom's grocery list and she bought one Saturday morning.

The Pumpkin Brownie Bars are really easy to make; mix together the first group of ingredients by hand or with a mixer. Take out one cup of the mixed batter and set it aside in a bowl. Add the chocolate, butter, oil & pumpkin puree to the main batter and mix some more. Spread in a buttered 9 x 13 pan.

In the bowl with the extra cup of batter, add pumpkin puree, oil & spices and spread it over the top of the brownie layer. Sprinkle chocolate chips over the whole top.

Bake at 350 for 35 – 45 minutes and be sure to leave them in the oven long enough so they get cooked all the way through in the middle. Great Grandma had made a note that the nutmeg was optional. I wanted them to have a nice pumpkin dessert flavor so I added it.

On Saturday afternoon, when the bars were cool, I cut them into twelve sections and I wrapped each bar in a small piece of plastic to keep them clean.

When I got to Emma's house, on the corner where we were setting up the bake sale, Nick and Max were already there moving a table under the big oak tree. Nick had made chocolate chip cookies, Max had made peanut butter cookies and Emma had made white cupcakes with chocolate frosting and sprinkles.

Emma's dad suggested we have some change in a small box, in case someone came by with larger bills. He loaned us a roll of quarters that equaled $10 as well as $10 worth of dollar bills. At the end of the sale, we would pay him back his $20 loan first, and then we could count our money.

That afternoon started slowly with a few neighbor kids stopping by to see what we were doing and rushing home for fifty cents to buy a dessert. We had a family of four stop and buy six items so they could share with their grandparents after dinner. My mom and dad came by and bought four cookies. Then a big surprise happened. Mrs. Smith from the ladies garden club drove up to drop off some plants for Emma's mom. She came to the table and bought one of my pumpkin brownie bars. She stood right there, ate it and listened as we told her our plans for the money.

"You know," she said. "I'm meeting with the business owners along Main Street tonight to plan out the Pumpkin Spooktacular and I'm going to take them a treat." She bought the remaining eleven pumpkin brownie bars and went on her way.

We closed up shop and sorted out the money. First we counted out the money in our little box. The total amount in the box was $40.

We set aside $20 and paid back Emma's dad first. There was $20 profit left after we paid back the loan. We made plans to go to the store and use our $20 to buy costume supplies after school on "Winner".

We had eight dessert items left so we each picked out two desserts for ourselves and headed home.

CHAPTER 2

Wednesday is early release from school so Max, Emma, Nick and I headed for the Main Street General Store. Mr. & Mrs. Patch have owned the store for as long as I can remember and they sell some of my favorite things.

In the back, by the big barrels of flour, sugar and oats, they have a shelf with collectible piggy banks. When I was five, my grandpa gave me one dollar worth of quarters and told me to "save it for a rainy day". I looked outside and it was raining so I asked him if I could spend it. He laughed and said "No,' save it for a rainy day' means to save it for when you really need it." I wasn't sure when I would need those four quarters, so I put them in a sock and tucked them away in a drawer.

About a week later I was at the General Store with my grandpa and spotted the cutest ceramic kitten "piggy bank". It was painted black with white paws. I showed it to my grandpa and he decided I needed a place to store my "rainy day" money. He bought it when I wasn't looking and surprised me with it for Christmas.

I put all four quarters in the "kitty bank" that Christmas and every year, my grandpa gives me another dollar. It has become our little game. One year he gave me ten dimes. The next year he gave me twenty nickels and last year he gave me 100 pennies. That black and white kitty bank was the first in my collection of "kitty banks" and it was my start in saving money.

My real full name is Catherine, but my family calls me Cat. I like having a short name. When I learned to read and write, Cat was an easy name to learn. I used to make up little stories and write small books.

One year our orange tabby cat gave birth to a litter of kittens. There were three kittens, one orange and two black. One of the black kittens had white paws. I would draw pictures of the kittens and make up little adventure stories. I called the book "Cat's Kittens". I thought it was a hilarious pun, since it sounded like they were my kittens, but also they were Mama Cat's kittens. When I saw the ceramic kitty bank, it reminded me of the little black kitten with the white paws that we named "Mittens".

Through the years, Mr. & Mrs. Patch have brought in other kitty banks to the General Store and because I love kittens, I started to collect kitty banks.

My second kitty bank was of a sweet orange tabby cat. She had swirls of white under her chin that made her look like she was licking up milk or vanilla ice cream. I decided that since the black and white kitty bank was for savings, this bank would be for things I wanted like books, craft supplies, birthday presents or just general things I needed in town. Whenever I would earn money raking leaves for my neighbors, or helping watch Emma's little brother, I would put half of the money in my Rainy Day Savings black and white kitty bank and half of it in my Personal Fund orange kitty bank.

On my last birthday, my brother gave me a new all white kitty bank. This one is special, because the cat has black eyelashes and soft looking long white hair. I decided this would be a special bank where I would save up donations. I like to give to the cat rescue organization that takes care of lost or sick cats. Once a month I add up how much I have made in chores and odd jobs and take ten percent and move it over to the special Donation white kitty bank.

When the four of us stopped by the General Store to buy supplies for our costumes Mr. & Mrs. Patch were there. Mr. Patch has a workshop in the back where he puts fabric on chairs and couches. Mrs. Patch stitches up matching pillows. They have bins of fabric pieces for quilts and projects.

We chose two different colors of fabric from the bins. One was a large piece that had a red background with big white dots all over it. Because it was red, it would work for our Christmas songs and for other holidays like Valentine's Day and the 4th of July. We also picked out a multi-color fabric with all of the colors of the rainbow in a swirl pattern.

On the left side of the store there is a big old gold mirror above a desk. The desk has drawers and shelves on top of it with items for sale. Mr. Patch added three round light bulbs on top and around each side of the mirror. It made the display look like an old fashioned make-up chair in the backstage of a theater. My friends and I love it because not only do they have regular makeup, lotions, shampoos and soaps, but one full drawer is dedicated to Halloween type makeup. There were little pots of colored face paint in white, blue, red and orange. We decided to buy a box that had six colors in it, so we could paint eyes and eyebrows on our chins for the show.

We headed home for "Winner" and spent some time working on the costumes. It was a busy day. Little did I know that in three days, what I thought was busy was going to seem like nothing.

CHAPTER 3

I was home on Saturday working on a puzzle with my brother when the phone rang. "Hello" I answered.

"Is this Cat?" asked a woman's voice.

"Yes, this is Cat," I said.

"This is Mrs. Smith. I bought those delicious 'twinkle bars' at the bake sale last week."

I laughed to myself when she called them 'twinkle bars'. "Yes, I remember. Hello Mrs. Smith."

"Say listen Cat, I shared the bars with Mr. Adams at The Blue Moon Café and he just loved them. He would like to order a batch of bars from you for the Halloween Spooktacular event on October 31st."

I was stunned and really didn't know what to say. "Well sure, I guess I can make another batch of bars," I said.

"Wonderful!" exclaimed Mrs. Smith. "They would like to order five hundred bars."

I caught my breath. "That's a lot of bars" I managed to say.

"Yes it is," she said, but they are willing to pay you 50 cents per brownie. It might be a nice little business for you."

A business? I'd always loved the businesses on Main Street with their stores; Mr. & Mrs. Patch with their General Store, Mr. Adams and his son at The Blue Moon Café and the Hanson sister's hair salon, but I had never had a good idea for my own business, until now.

I told my family about my new baking business that night. My grandparents were over for Saturday dinner. After we were done playing games, my grandpa suggested I write down a business plan.

We took out a sheet of paper and I made a list of things I needed to start my own business.

"First," I said, I need to make a list of all the ingredients I will need. My recipe only makes 12 brownies."

Since the order was for 500 brownies, I would need to figure out how many batches to make. I divided 500 bars by 12 which came out to 41.67 batches. I rounded up to the nearest whole number which was 42 batches of brownies.

Then I wrote out a basic business plan for the Cat's Twinkle Bar business. I called them "Twinkle Bars" just like Mrs. Smith, because that made them sound special.

- Create ingredient list for 42 batches of bars
- Find pans to cook multiple batches of bars at the same time
- Decide how to wrap each brownie – plastic wrap or baggies
- Find a bigger oven or several ovens to use
- Find a few people to help me
- Talk to Mr. Adams to find out when to deliver the order
- Look for a way to transport the order to the café

I was really proud of my list and showed it to my mom and dad the next night at dinner. They were encouraging and had a few questions for me. My mom handed me the bowl of potatoes and asked, "Where are you going to get the ingredients?"

"Well," I said, "we can get them at the store on Saturday during our family grocery shopping trip, right?" I asked.

"Have you figured out the cost of your ingredients yet?" she asked. "I don't think that the ingredients for 42 batches of brownies will fit into our weekly grocery budget" she added kindly.

I hadn't considered that. "I could take my list with me on Saturday and walk around the store to price out the ingredients," I suggested.

"Great idea," my dad smiled. "That's one of the first principles of business, knowing your 'cost of goods sold'," he said.

"Cost of goods sold?" I asked.

"Yes," he said. "Every product that gets sold has a cost to it. For example this table we are sitting around came from Mr. Root's furniture store across town. He buys the tables from a manufacturing company that makes them for a certain "cost" and then he marks up the price of the table so he can make a profit. I do his accounting and I know that in the furniture business, his cost is usually about 50% of the final price of the table."

"How much was this table?" I asked.

"We bought this table last summer for $800," my mom chimed in. "I was so happy it matched the chairs we bought from him a few years ago."

"So if we paid $800 for the table, his cost from the manufacturer was $400," I said.

"Yes, that's right," my dad said. "He likely paid $400 to the Oak Furniture Company that makes the tables. They buy the raw wood, use their tools and workshop and pay their carpenters to make the tables. The Oak Furniture Company figures out how much it costs them to make a table and then sells the table wholesale for $400 to Mr. Root. Mr Root then marks them up to $800 so he can make a profit. Remember he has expenses at his store too like rent, electricity, employees, and advertising. He doesn't make a full profit of $400 when he sells it for $800, but if he knows his "cost of goods sold" on the table and he knows his expenses, he will make a profit on each table he sells.

"You know Cat," my brother piped up, "you are a lot like the Oak Furniture Company. You are the wholesale person making the pumpkin bars, just like they make the tables."

"Yes," my dad said, "so you need to figure out how much your ingredients and other supplies cost so you can make a profit, just like the Oak Table company does when they sell a table to Mr. Root. Once you sell a bar to Mr. Adams at The Blue Moon Café, then he will mark them up to make his profit."

So that is where I started – figuring out my "cost of goods sold".

I went to the grocery store with my mom and brother on Saturday and wrote down the cost of each ingredient. Then I spent the afternoon making a chart to show the breakdown of my costs.

For example, a dozen eggs cost $1.80. I divided $1.80 by 12 eggs in the carton to find out how much each egg cost, which was 15 cents. To make 42 batches of brownies, I already knew I needed 252 eggs, so I just multiplied 252 x .15 and found out it would cost $37.80 for the eggs.

I continued to do that for each item until I had a total cost. My dad showed me how to format a chart.

Ingredients	Price Per Unit	Total Units Needed	Total Price for 42 Batches
1 1/2 sticks butter	.25 each stick	63 sticks butter	$15.75
1 1/2 cup sugar	.20 per cup	63 cups sugar	$12.60
6 eggs	.15 each egg	252 eggs	$37.80
1 can (15 oz) pumpkin	.55 per can	42 cans pumpkin	$23.10
3 cups flour	.35 per cup	126 cups flour	$44.10
1 1/2 tsp cinnamon	.03 per tsp	63 tsp cinnamon	$1.89
1/4 tsp nutmeg	.01 per 1/4 tsp	10 1/2 tsp nutmeg	$.11 cents
3/4 tsp salt	.75 per box (less than 1 cent per batch)	31 1/2 tsp salt	$.75 cents
1/2 cup cocoa	.70 per cup	21 cups	$14.70
1/3 c. vegetable oil	.20 per cup	14 cups	$2.80
1 1/2 tsp vanilla	.03 per tsp	63 tsp	$1.89
1/3 bag choc. chips	.65 per bag	14 bags	$9.10
		TOTAL COST	$164.59

CHAPTER 4

Now that I had my cost for the ingredients list, I was feeling more confident. I showed it to my grandpa that night. "Well done Cat!" he said. "You're getting the hang of being a business owner."

"Are you ready for the next important number?" he asked.

"Sure," I said.

"Let's compare your numbers to how much the Café is going to pay you for each brownie," he encouraged.

I told him that Mrs. Smith said that the Café was going to buy each brownie from me for 50 cents.

"My total cost for all the ingredients is $164.59".I said.

I wrote down:

Total Cost of Ingredients = $164.59
42 batches x 12 bars per pan = 504 bars

Then I divided my cost of $164.59 by the number of bars which is 504 and that equals .33 cents per bar.

"Excellent!" Grandpa said. "Mr. Adams is going to pay you 50 cents per brownie. How much profit will you make?" he asked.

I did the math: .50 cents - .33 cents = .17 cents profit per bar

It wasn't a 50% profit, but it was a good start, I thought to myself.

"Are there any other costs for the brownies," he asked?

"Let me think," I said. "I need to figure out a few things like which ovens to use. I also need a few people to help me and figure out how to deliver the bars to the café. So, I started on those items next.

That Wednesday at Winner we had a Chin-a-kins rehearsal. We were working on two new songs for our holiday show in December. It was odd to be singing Christmas songs before Halloween, but we wanted to have our routine memorized and our costumes ready early. We decided to do a medley of three songs. We started off as four elves, became four reindeer and ended up as four angels.

My mom gave us some brown felt and we sat around the basement cutting out our antlers. "How's the dessert business Cat?" Nick asked.

"Yeah I can't wait to come over and get some samples while you are baking," said Max.

"Well" I said, "I named my business 'Cat's Twinkle Bars'". I also figured out how much it will cost to make 42 batches of bars. I just don't know how I am going to get them all cooked, cooled, wrapped up and delivered on time" I said. "I made a batch this morning to practice my recipe. It takes me 30 minutes to make them, 30 minutes to bake them and then they need at least an hour to cool before I can even think of wrapping them. I'm worried about how to get them all done in time."

"You should try the system of mass production that was used by Henry Ford when he started building cars." All three of us stopped and looked up at Max.

"What are you talking about," I asked?

"In my after-school Boy Scout troop on Mondays, we are building model cars," he said. "It was taking too long to get them done during our meetings so our scout leader told us about Henry Ford. He was the man who started building cars faster than others because he broke the process down to specific jobs for each of the workers. The workers got really good at their jobs, so they got them done more efficiently."

"There are ten of us in the scout troop," he continued. "We decided to break the car building process down into ten different steps. We each put our car in a shoebox with our name on it and then put the boxes in a big bag. One guy takes them all home each night. The first was Tommy. He was really fast at putting the windows in the cars. He was a little ahead of the rest of us and had figured out the knack of snapping them into place. He took them home Monday night and brought them all back to school on Tuesday. Aaron took them home on Tuesday and is putting all the decals on the sides. I get them on Saturday and am going to install the tires. I already took the hubs and wheels home and glued them together. I can pop each tire on, in about an hour on Saturday. By our Monday meeting they will be almost done."

Emma and I glanced at each other. "That sounds great Max, but how do we apply mass production to pumpkin bars? We can't each take home a few ingredients?" I said.

"Well first you need a work force, or at least more than one person, to make all the bars," said Max.

"I'll help," said Emma.

"Me too" said Nick "as long as I can eat the bad ones."

I laughed. "Hopefully there won't be many bad ones. But maybe we can make a few extra batches so you could each have some to eat yourselves."

They all agreed to help, so we devised a plan.

We each have one oven at home. We divided 42 batches by the 4 of us but that wasn't an even number, so increased our batches to 44 and calculated it would be simpler if we each made 11 batches. By making 44 total batches, we would have two extra batches for any problems that might arise or to use as extras for my friends to take home when we were done.

I adjusted my ingredient list to account for the new quantities. My new "cost of goods sold" for 44 batches would be $172.67. I was still only selling Mr. Adams 500 bars since we were keeping some as extra. I divided $172.67 by 500 which made the cost of each bar .34 cents.

I learned from my dad that this was called a "variable cost" since the cost would change depending on how many bars I made. In this case, it was totally worth the cost of two extra batches to have so much help.

My friends and I also realized it would go a lot faster if we each made two batches of brownies at once. We each had bowls in our kitchen large enough to mix up a double batch and then we could pour the batter into two pans. I asked them to check to see if they each had two 13 x 9 pans in their kitchen. If not I would borrow pans from my grandparents or other neighbors.

We agreed to divide into two teams; Nick and Max and me and Emma. Nick and Max would make a first double batch at Nick's house. While the bars were cooling off, they would go to Max's house and make a second batch. While the second batch was cooling, they would go back to Nick's and cut the bars into sections, wrap up the individual brownies and make a new batch. Emma and I would do the same. We would be efficient and have fun helping each other.

Fortunately, Halloween was on a Sunday this year. We could make all the bars on Saturday and deliver them on Sunday morning. I was getting excited. My business was starting to take shape, but I still had one big obstacle and one big surprise coming my way.

CHAPTER 5

I still didn't know how I was going to pay for the supplies I needed. I had my kitty banks, but the total money in all of them didn't add up to the amount I needed to buy the ingredients.

On Friday when I got home from school, my mom told me I had missed a call from Mr. Adams at The Blue Moon Café. His number was on the board by the phone so I dialed it up. A big booming voice said "Café Blue, how are you?"

I smiled. "Hello Mr. Adams, it's Cat Casey calling you back."

"Oh yes, the pumpkin brownie baker! How good of you to return my call." He continued, "Miss Baker would you be able to stop by the cafe tomorrow afternoon so we can confirm the arrangements for our order?"

"Yes sir, I can come by about 3pm. Will that work?"

"Delightful!" said Mr. Adams. "See you tomorrow!" he boomed.

On Saturday, my brother and I rode our bikes into town to return some library books and get our haircuts at the Hanson Scissors Salon. The Hanson sisters had been cutting our hair since we were two years old and knew us like family.

"There she is," smiled Patty. "The Twinkle Bar girl".

I grinned "How did you know?" I asked.

"Oh there is very little that goes on in this town that we don't hear about. Mrs. Adams had her hair done the Monday after your bars found their way to the meeting at the cafe" she said. "She told us that Ms. Smith had brought the most delicious treats for the meeting and they were going to order a big batch for the special day."

"That's right," I told her. They ordered five-hundred!"

"Five hundred?" asked her sister Lindsey. "How will you ever manage an order that big?"

"I have the mass production all worked out with my "Winner" friends," I said, "but I am still trying to figure out how to pay for all the ingredients."

"Yes, that is a challenge," said Patty after I told her how I figured out the total amount of money I needed.

"How are you going to decorate the bars?" asked Lindsey as she cut the hair over my brother's eyes.

"Decorate?" I asked. "I guess I was just going to wrap them in plastic wrap," I said.

"Oh no," said Patty and Lindsey at the same time.

"You must give them your own signature style," Patty said.

"Why don't you head over to the General Store after your haircut and look around at their displays. Maybe that will give you some ideas for your packaging," said Lindsey.

After our haircuts we had about thirty minutes before I was going over to the cafe. My brother rode off to the park where a group of kids were playing frisbee. I walked into the General Store. Mrs. Patch and her mother were behind the shop counter and greeted me kindly. "What can we do for you today dear?" Mrs. Patch asked.

"I came in for some ideas on how to decorate my Pumpkin Twinkle Bars for the Halloween Spooktacular" I told them. "The Hanson sisters said I need a signature look, but I don't quite know what to do."

The women glanced at each other and smiled. "Take a look around and let us know if you find any ideas." Mrs. Patch said.

I spent twenty minutes looking around. I even took a few minutes to look at the kitty banks, but nothing really came to mind. I liked how the soaps had a ribbon around them. I liked the round brown price tag on each item for sale, but I wasn't sure how that would look on a twinkle bar.

I waved goodbye on my way out and popped across the street to the café. The front steps already had carved pumpkins out on display and there were bales of hay on the porch. Settled upon the hay was the cutest black kitten I had ever seen. She just blinked her eyes and went back to sleep. That's it, I thought, "black cat".

Mr. Adams was ringing up a customer so I sat down at the counter to wait. When he was done he turned to me. "Ah Miss Baker, right on time, how considerate. Let's have a 'cup-a' while we have our meeting". He poured himself a cup of coffee (or as he says a "cup-a") and me a cup of cocoa.

"We are very pleased to order those delicious brownie bars for the Halloween Spooktakular. How are your plans coming for our order of five-hundred?" he asked.

"I figured out my 'cost of goods sold' and have a plan for mass production" I told him, hoping my use of business terms would make me sound professional.

"Ah, yes indeed" he nodded seriously. "Very important to get your details in order."

"Will the bars be the same size as the ones we tasted when Ms. Smith brought them to us?" he asked.

"Yes" I told him, "I make twelve brownies out of each batch".

"Will they be wrapped individually like before?" he asked.

"Yes" I said with a smile, "they are officially called "Pumpkin Twinkle Bars" and they will have a special decoration on each one."

"Excellent!" said Mr. Adams. "Then all we have left is to confirm our order with a contract." He picked up a piece of paper and handed it to me. "This is a purchase order," he said. "It is our request in writing for the order. At the bottom we have noted that the bars are to be delivered Sunday morning between 7am – 8am, before we open."

"Yes, Mr. Adams," I said. "I can provide five-hundred twinkle bars by 7am on the 31st.

"Excellent Miss Baker, he said, and handed me the purchase order. "Now there is one more thing," he said. "I would like to make a deposit for the order. I will pay you half of the amount we owe now and the balance when you make the delivery."

My eyes opened wide but I didn't miss a beat. "Yes sir, that would be excellent," I said, using his "excellent" word back.

He walked over to the cash register and pulled out $125. He made a note on the purchase order of the amount. We both wrote our initials next to it as a confirmation.

With a wink and a smile he was off to serve the next customer. I was off to my bike with the money I needed to buy the ingredients and get started on my secret plan for packaging the twinkle bars.

I went straight home and found a metal box with a latch on it in the garage. I put the $125 deposit and purchase order in the box for safekeeping, then I headed to the kitchen to help my mom with dinner.

Before I washed my hands I called my grandma and asked her to bring a box of craft supplies she has in her extra bedroom. After dinner my mom, dad, grandpa and brother settled in around the table to play cards. My grandma and I went into the living room and worked for a couple of hours cutting and prepping my decorations. I didn't let anyone else see them. This was a fun surprise.

The next week came and went with school and Wednesday Winner. We skipped Chin-a-kins practice and I showed Nick, Max and Emma how to bake the twinkle bars. After dinner they were cool enough to cut into rectangles and wrap with plastic wrap. It was good practice.

Nick cut the batch and Max started wrapping the bars. They decided Nick was a neater wrapper, so they switched roles and Max cut the rest. It was important for the brownies to be the same size so I had made a template. First they had to cut the pan of brownies in half the long way and then cut each side into six even bars. I showed them the decoration for finishing off each one like a little package. They were really impressed. "It looks like it came from a professional bakery," said Emma.

The next day my dad and I went grocery shopping to get all of the ingredients. My grandpa had been watching the newspaper and found a sale on eggs at a grocery a few miles away. The eggs were on sale for only 60 cents per dozen which made them .05 cents each. Since eggs were one of the most expensive ingredients in my recipe, it would be worth getting them at the sale price. By saving $26.40 on eggs, I would be able to make that much more in profit.

When we got home I divided the ingredients into four boxes so we could split everything between the four kitchens. The eggs went into the refrigerator in four stacks. We would put them on the top of the boxes when we delivered them to each house on Saturday.

The countdown was on and all we needed to do was execute my plan.

CHAPTER 6

Saturday morning started off with a delivery of supplies to my friend's houses. We loaded the boxes in the back of my dad's car and carried the ingredients into each kitchen. While I was in the kitchen I made sure they had the two baking pans needed for making the double batch of bars. Emma's and Max's house each had two of the correct size pans. Nick only had one, so I borrowed a pan from my grandparents and delivered it with the box of supplies.

Each friend had set out a mixer, a bowl, measuring cups, spoons and aprons. Our families had talked about my business plan on "Winner" and agreed to meet at the Old Stone Pizza House for dinner that night. That we could use the kitchens without interruptions all day.

Nick and Max started at Nick's house on their first batch of bars. Emma and I started at her house since I was already there delivering supplies.

We have a set of walkie-talkies that we use when we are out riding bikes or playing in the woods. We used them to talk back and forth as we got started.

Once the first batch was cooked and out of the oven, we set the pans on the counter to cool. Emma and I headed to my house and started on batch number two. Max called us on the walkie-talkie and told us they were at his house on their second batch as well.

When batch number two was set out to cool, Emma and I headed back to her house. We cut both pans of bars according to my template and wrapped them in plastic. I washed the two pans while Emma started mixing the next set of ingredients. We put the third batch in the oven, washed the mixing bowl and measuring cups and started on the decorations.

I had made five hundred round tags by paper punching light brown craft paper into circles. On each tag my grandma and I stamped the image of a black cat arching his back, while standing next to a pumpkin.

I remembered my grandma had the stamp in her craft kit from a few years back. Since my name is Cat and the stamp had a picture of a Halloween cat, it seemed like the perfect way to decorate the Pumpkin Twinkle Bars.

I punched a small hole at the top of the tag and we ran a string through the tag and tied it around each bar. The tags laid flat right in the center and the string was tied off with a bow.

We used the big box my dad and I had used to deliver the ingredients and lined the brownies in the box on their sides. Our first batch of twenty-four bars was complete.

We called Nick & Max and they were almost done with packaging their first batch as well. All we had to do was keep baking ...but a few problems came our way.

Nick and Max put in batch number four and set the timer. They went outside to throw the baseball and didn't hear the timer when it beeped. The bars ended up in the oven for about 5 or 6 minutes too long.

They called me on the walkie-talkie and I ran over to look at them while Emma kept our production line going. I decided the overcooked brownies were ok to keep but the bars on the corners were a little too crispy. We put those eight bars in a separate box to use as the "extras" we were keeping for ourselves.

Emma and I ran into trouble later in the day when she dropped a carton of eggs on the floor as she was getting them out of the refrigerator. The eggs cracked immediately as they hit the floor and made a big sticky mess. Fortunately there were only four eggs in the carton. Her mom had extra eggs in the refrigerator and she let us use them as a replacement.

It was a lot of responsibility to produce and be in charge of getting five hundred brownies all done in one day, but we did it. By the end of the day we had four boxes of bars. The brownies were stacked in the boxes in neat rows with cardboard in between them so they wouldn't smash each other.

My dad helped me pick up each large box and load it into his car. We realized it would be easiest to leave the boxes in the car overnight so they would be ready for delivery the next morning.

The four of us were tired and hungry when we got to dinner at Old Stone. We ate pizza, played the pinball machine in the back room and shared the "extra" twinkle bars with our families as a thank you for letting us use the kitchens. Max and Nick volunteered to eat the crispy ones.

The next morning my dad drove me to The Blue Moon Café. He pulled the car up behind the café where the vendors make their deliveries. My brother's friend Ryan was making a delivery of eggs from his family's farm. Mr. Adams' son was in charge of receiving deliveries. We brought in the four big boxes of Pumpkin Twinkle Bars and I showed him the purchase order. He pulled out a stack of cash and counted out the balance owed me of $125.

And that was it. The first order in Cat's Twinkle Bar business was delivered. I went back home and put the money in my metal box. Then I went downstairs for breakfast. I realized with all the planning and production of the dessert business, I hadn't finished putting together my Halloween costume.

We always go to the Halloween Spooktacular as a family. Sometimes we dress up in costumes that match or are similar to each other. Two years ago we all went as pirates. The year before when we went as garden gnomes. This year my mom and dad decided to do the standard witch and wizard costumes and my brother was going as a king with a long red cape.

I was also doing my own costume. Mr. Adams had sparked an idea when he called me "Miss Baker." Even though my name is Cat Casey, he called me Miss Baker because I was baking Pumpkin Twinkle Bars.

I took some thin white material and stapled it to a white headband and made it fluff up like a baker's hat. I put on a white shirt with a white apron and filled a small basket with a rolling pin, some cookie cutters and a few measuring cups.

My final touch was a piece of orange fabric I found in our sewing supplies. I cut it in a long strip and used my grandma's Halloween cat stamp to decorate the length of the fabric. The ink dried quickly and was ready by the time I tied the scarf around my neck, just like a baker.

CHAPTER 7

The town was glowing when we parked at the school and walked down Main Street. There were carved pumpkins in every store window. The Hanson Scissors Salon had four pumpkins sitting on chairs in the window. Each pumpkin had on a wig and a hat.

The General Store had pumpkins in their windows too. One window had an old kitchen table with a large pumpkin in the center of the table. There were at least a dozen mini pumpkins on the table, chairs, and floor. Each one was carved with circles and stars and was glowing from the strands of lights.

Their other window had a small stuffed witch sitting on the floor, holding a glass bowl full of tiny fake spiders. The bowl was tipped over to look like her spiders had spilled. There were lights around her and her cobweb. It reminded me of a scene in a fairy tale.

I found Emma, Nick and Max at the Hardware Store where there was a maze of hay bales in the back lot. We made our way through the maze after a few wrong turns and laughed all the way back to the center of town.

The Blue Moon Café was the highlight of the Halloween Spooktacular. Mr. Adams had hired several carpenters to work overnight. They had turned the café into a series of small rooms. One room had one of the school teachers dressed up like a wizard surrounded by beautiful rocks and stones. Another room had a player piano playing, with no person sitting on the stool. There were glowing pumpkins all around the front porch and small carved pumpkins across the length of the cafe' counter.

Our eyes got used to the dimly lit rooms. When we came around to the side door, there was a folding table covered with orange and black checkered fabric. Right in the middle of the table was a big basket full of my bars. The café's kitchen was shut down for the evening and all they were selling was coffee, cocoa and "Cat's Pumpkin Twinkle Bars."

I couldn't believe it. "Look" I whispered and my friends just stopped in their tracks.

Mr. Adams had not only given me my first big order, he had featured my bars right up front for all of his customers.

"Ahhh, Miss Baker" boomed Mr. Adams, jolting us from the quiet. "It looks like you are dressed perfectly for your role."

I smiled and nodded as he handed each of us a "cup-a" cocoa.

"On the house for your good work," he said. "The Pumpkin Twinkle Bars have been so popular, I would like you to come by next week so I can order a new flavor for the upcoming holiday season," he said. And with that he turned to his next customer.

We walked out on to Main Street and I was in business again.

Wow, he really loved the twinkle bars," Nick said.

"Yeah, that was amazing," said Max. "You really started a great business."

From that day forward I became known as Cat Casey with the Twinkle Bar Business. I met with Mr. Adams the following week and he requested I make brownies with a mint flavor. I tried a few recipes and developed a regular chocolate brownie with crushed candy canes on top. I named them Holiday Twinkle Bars.

Mr. Adams now orders from me four times per year. I make him my special Red Velvet Brownies ("I Love" Twinkle Bars) for Valentine's Day. My deluxe Red, White and Blue Bars (Celebration Twinkle Bars) are for the 4th of July. These are my dad's favorite, with marshmallows and red and blue sprinkles on top. Mr. Adams has also helped me with my production. He lets me use his big commercial oven the night before each holiday, where I can bake twice as fast.

Before the week was over, I took out my metal box and sorted my money. In total, Mr. Adams had paid me 50 cents per brownie for a total net revenue of $250.

My cost of goods sold was $146.27. It was less than my original calculations because I saved money on the eggs.

I subtracted my "cost of goods sold" from my net revenue. That gave me a gross profit of $103.73.

I set aside $5 to give to my dad for his help with deliveries and gas for the car. I also bought a new roll of plastic wrap for $1.50 and a bundle of string for .50 cents for my family's kitchen. I had used the supplies we had in the pantry, but wanted my business to cover all the costs for my business.

I got out three envelopes and put $5 in each for Max, Nick & Emma. It was important to pay them for helping me with the production. I would be talking to them about helping me again on my next order and wanted them to know how much I appreciated their help.

I set out my kitty banks in front of me and divided my profit into five piles.

- First was my Black Kitty Rainy Day Fund. I put in 25% of the profit or $20.43 in the bank.
- The second was my Orange Tabby for my Personal Funds. That was another 25% or $20.43.
- The third was my metal box. I put 25% into my Twinkle Bar Business Account of $20.43. I will use this account for business supplies like practice recipes, extra pans and bowls.
- The fourth was 10% into White Kitty for my next Donation to the animal shelter of $8.18.
- The fifth was a new Grey Kitty bank I ordered. It has a silver bell around its neck that makes a "twinkle" sound. I divided out 15% or $12.26 and put it in the new bank. I call it my "Business Seed Money". I will save 15% every time I have an order so that one day I can open up my own Twinkle Bar Bakery, right on Main Street.

The Little Books of Big Business series follows four friends in Main Town USA on their journey into business. Cat, Emma, Nick & Max each start their own businesses and learn key principles along the way. This series is perfect for anyone ages 5 to 105 who aspires to be an entrepreneur.

Book #1

Meet Cat Casey...the girl who turns her grandmother's brownie recipe into a business. With the help of family and friends, she learns business principles like "cost of goods sold", mass production and making a profit. Learn along with Cat as she launches her delicious Twinkle Bar business.

Find the next book, activities & worksheets:

LittleBooksofBigBusiness.com

Author's Note: The Little Books of Big Business series is intentionally set in a small town where characters can interact with local business owners. While this may not be as easy in today's world, kids can still experiment with business principles in their own neighborhood, school or local communities. The story purposely leaves out technology like computers and cell phones. Just as it is important to learn to calculate math with pencil and paper before relying on a calculator, so it is with writing up an invoice, tracking your receipts in an envelope or receiving cash and counting back the change.

About the Author

Mara Williams is a Professionally Certified Coach and Business Coaching Specialist. She is passionate about teaching women and kids about money and business principles through stories and fun activities.

SuccessStreetCoaching.com and SuccessStreetBusiness.com

CPSIA information can be obtained
at www.ICGtesting.com
Printed in the USA
LVHW080734051121
702404LV00005B/113